To my late grandmother, Laura Almira (Young) Malpass, my aunt, Mary Leone (Scherick) Malpass, and to the late Dave Goodeman and Kyle Marshall, who together, at great personal risk, tried to rescue a Labrador Retriever.

S.M.M.

To Shelby, Autumn, Beth,
Happy Trails,
Suzanne M. Malpass

With love,
Grammy Cook
2014

A Lab's Tale

Story © 2012 by Suzanne M. Malpass, suzanne@straddlebooks.com
Illustrations © 2012 by Trish Morgan, trish@peachbloomhill.com

PRT0412A

Printed in the United States

ISBN-13: 9781937406684
ISBN-10: 1937406687

www.mascotbooks.com

Suzanne M. Malpass

Illustrated by Trish Morgan

A Lab's Tale

"Smoky just stole another chicken," said the voice on the phone.

Grandma Laura sank into her chair with a discouraged sigh. "Oh my, Harriet, I'm so sorry. What am I going to do with him? I can't seem to keep that dog from running away. This afternoon I'll come over and pay for the chicken. I really am sorry."

For many years the tall, ginger-haired grandma had lived a quiet, respectable life in East Jordan, a small town on Lake Charlevoix in Northern Michigan. She enjoyed listening to the Detroit Tigers on the radio, reading poetry and playing Scrabble. Her namesake granddaughter claimed Grandma cheated at Scrabble. The other grandchildren refused to believe that their oh-so-proper grandma would ever do such a thing.

Every day Grandma Laura wore a dress and sensible shoes. After church on Sunday, she made delicious chicken or ham dinners for her nearby children and grandchildren.

With her oldest grandson, Billy, she would sometimes walk over to the Sunset Hill Cemetery to put fresh flowers on Grandpa Will's grave.

Grandma Laura's quiet life was turned upside down by a fateful phone call from her youngest son. "Mom, Mary saw an ad in the newspaper about a railroad welding job in Anchorage. I landed it, so we're heading up there," Glen announced.

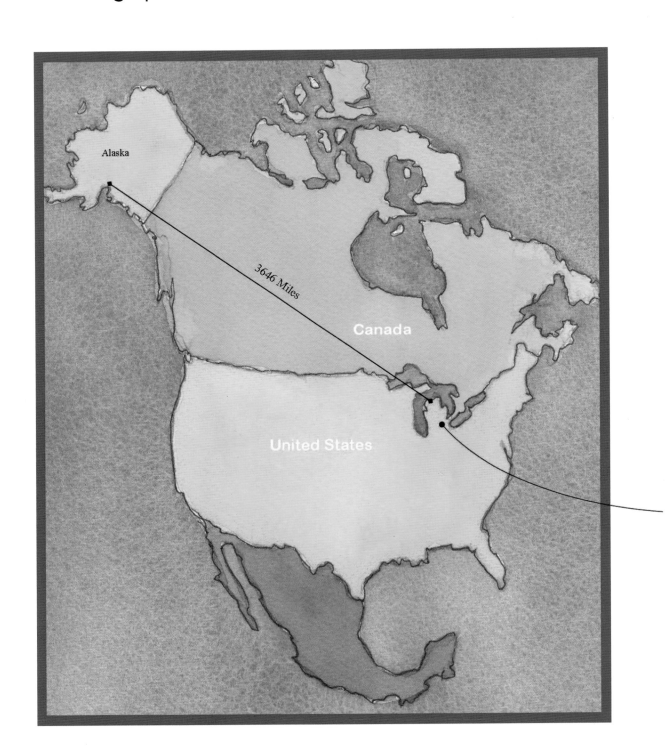

"Alaska is awfully far away," Grandma said.

"I know, but welding is what I trained for and what I like to do. There is a problem, though. We have to fly separately on military transports and no pets are allowed. So, could we leave Smoky with you for a while, Mom?"

Grandma agreed to take care of the black lab, though she had no idea what that would mean. Knowing their dog was in good hands, Glen and his wife, Mary, took off for Alaska.

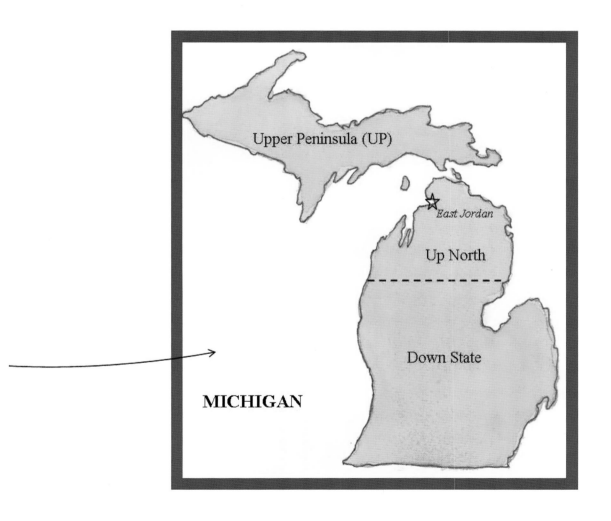

Since that decision, Smoky had become somewhat of a tourist attraction in East Jordan. More than once, a conversation like this took place at the lake. "Look at that, Ethel! There's a dog swimming across the lake with a live chicken in its mouth!"

"Earl, are you kidding me?"

"Please, just turn around and take a look, Ethel."

"My stars, I never thought I'd see such a thing! Wait 'til I tell the girls back home."

In many ways Smoky was a perfectly normal, friendly black lab. His body was strong and muscular, with webbed paws for swimming and an inky black water-resistant coat. But… beyond that… normal became unusual.

First, Smoky had a white star on his tongue. Second, he wagged not only his tail, but also his entire hindquarters! Last and most notably, the lab had an unending curiosity about other animals and wanted to be friends with all of them. Grandma Laura had to bathe him in tomato juice several times because he got too close to a skunk.

Once in the spring and twice in the summer, she had to take Smoky to the vet to have porcupine quills pulled out of his nose and mouth. While he worked, Doc Porter wondered aloud, "Will this dog never learn? These barbed quills burn like fire. Most dogs only tangle with a porcupine once."

Smoky's attempts at friendship caused other problems, too. He often tried to rescue the grandchildren when they were swimming in the lake and in absolutely no danger.

Jane and the others would yell, "No, Smoky, no!"

Grandma Laura would try to command or lure him back to where she stood on the beach.

Sometimes a stinky problem would crop up because Smoky didn't always limit his attention to live animals. Whenever there was a chance, he would roll in dead fish that washed up on shore.

Worst of all for Grandma Laura were the days when Smoky ran away and swam across the south arm of Lake Charlevoix. On the other side, he would steal a chicken from someone's yard and swim back with it in his mouth. These "chicken days" upset Grandma so much, that friends had offered more than once to take the dog off her hands.

Grandma always refused. "No, thank you," she'd say. "Smoky isn't even my dog. I'm just keeping him for Glen and Mary."

The real reason she declined was because she liked Smoky so much! In many ways, he was the perfect companion for a lonely widow. He slept quietly on the rug in front of the fireplace while she knit mittens for her grandchildren, read or did crossword puzzles.

Whenever Smoky roused himself and wandered over by her chair, Grandma would set down whatever she was doing and fondly pat his head.

His deep bark was the perfect warning system when anyone unexpected came near her home.

"I just feel safer with Smoky by my side," Grandma often remarked. She and the black lab passed many happy months together in relative calm--

except for the chicken, skunk, porcupine and dead fish incidents.

Then winter arrived, which happens very early up north. (Once it even snowed on the Fourth of July!) By late December, not even Smoky could swim across the lake because it was frozen over. Once the ice was thick enough, if there was no snow on top, people could skate on it. When it got even thicker, fish shanties appeared, then fresh smelt and perch could be part of winter meals.

A frozen Lake Charlevoix adds to the beautiful winter landscape up north. But the ice can be deadly dangerous! Not all of it has the same thickness. Especially near the shoreline, where a natural spring feeds into the lake, the ice is likely to crack and break. If it does, a dog, a deer or even a person can end up in the icy water. Toward the end of the winter, the ice starts breaking up and is even less reliable.

One day in early April, Smoky tried to make friends with some Canadian geese that had forgotten to migrate south for the winter. Each time he ran toward them, they would fly to a different spot on the ice. After the first few chases, the geese landed on some very unstable ice.

As the lab bounded after his new friends, the ice began to fail. Cracks radiated out from each place his big paws landed. Then, all of a sudden, the ice broke and dumped poor Smoky into the frigid water! He struggled desperately to get back on top of the ice, but it just kept breaking.

Sometime later, two local fishermen arrived to check out the ice conditions and came upon a miniature schnauzer pacing the shore and barking frantically. As they looked out at the lake, one of the men spotted something thrashing around in a dark hole in the ice.

"Dave, look! It's a dog!" Kyle pointed out excitedly. "We've got to help him!"

"Yeah, but we've got to be really careful," Dave said. "If we fall into that water it could be the end of us, too."

With a pounding heart, Kyle started out toward the dog. After a few uncertain steps, he broke through the ice. Luckily, he was able to keep going. When he got near the struggling lab, he reached out his hand. Smoky lunged toward it and Kyle was able to grab a paw. Very slowly he started dragging the exhausted animal to shallower water.

In the meantime, Grandma Laura was out searching for her wayward companion. She arrived at Dutchman's Bay shortly before man and dog reached the shore. Both were achingly cold.

Grandma thanked the men wholeheartedly and invited them to her house to warm up. She explained, "The little dog is Sophie, my daughter's dog. They live right over there on the north side of the bay," said Grandma as she pointed to the right. "Smoky and Sophie play together all the time."

"That explains why the schnauzer was barking so wildly-- her buddy was in danger," said Dave.

Later in front of a sparkling fire, Grandma Laura, Kyle, and Dave warmed up with hot chocolate and homemade raisin-topped sugar cookies. Grandma was so relieved that Smoky was safe, she even gave half a cookie (but no raisins) to each dog. The men laughed as they heard about all the trouble Smoky had gotten into. Realizing that the lab was unlikely to ever change, Grandma Laura vowed to stop worrying about him and just enjoy the fact that Smoky had come to live with her.

The End

Many thanks to Pat, Carl and Lisa Bloom, to my husband, Jeff Rogers, and to my stellar supporters: Heather Baker, Marsha Beck, Evelyn Malpass, Tina Malpass, Karen Smith and, most especially, Anne Houser.

Have a book idea?
Contact us at:

Mascot Books
560 Herndon Parkway
Suite 120
Herndon, VA 20170

info@mascotbooks.com | www.mascotbooks.com